HARRY HELPS OUT!

Written by Thomas James

Illustrated by Veronica Buffington

Troll Associates

Today is Saturday.

**It is a day for helping.
Harry is going to help his
mother and father.**

There is a lot to do.
Harry's mother is going
to clean the house.

Harry's father
is going to wash
the car.

What is Harry going to do?

"How can I help?" asks Harry.

"You can help me clean.
You can help me vacuum
the living room rug."

It is fun to vacuum!

"Whirrr" goes the vacuum.

"Whooosh" goes the dust.

Here is the cat.

The cat likes to sleep on something soft.

The cat is sleeping on the rug.

Here is Harry.

"I have vacuumed the rug," he says.

"Now, I want to clean something else."

WHAT IS HARRY THINKING?

"What shall I vacuum
now?" says Harry.
"I want to clean
something else."

Here is Harry's dog, Sherman.

Harry looks at Sherman.

WHAT IS HARRY THINKING?

"Sherman likes to be clean," says Harry.

Sherman barks and barks.
Sherman hates the vacuum!

Here is Harry's mother again.

"Thank you for cleaning
the rug, Harry. But I don't think
the dog and cat like to be vacuumed.
Perhaps your father would like some help."

"That is a good idea," says Harry.
"I like to help Father."

Harry's father is washing the car.

"May I help you, Father?"
asks Harry.

"Yes, Harry, you can help me
by turning on the hose,"
says his father.

Harry turns on the hose,
but he forgets to hold onto the hose.
Water is squirting all over.

Water is squirting Harry's father.

"Turn off the water!"
shouts Harry's father.
"Turn off the water,
Harry!"

"I am sorry, Father," says Harry.

"That's all right, Harry. Here, you can use this bucket and sponge to wash the car."

Harry's father goes in the house to put on some dry clothes.

Now Harry is washing the car. He is so happy that he forgets where the bucket is.

Watch out, Harry!

SPLASH!

Poor Harry!
He has put his foot
right in the bucket
of soapy water.

"Oh dear," says Harry,
"now I've done it again!"

Here comes
Harry's father.

His father helps pull his foot out of the bucket.

"Better put some dry shoes on, Harry," says his father.

"Perhaps you can help
Mother now."

In the house, Harry puts on dry shoes.

"I am ready to help you, Mother," says Harry. "I have
finished helping Father.
What are you doing?"

"I am baking a cake," says his mother.
"You can help me stir the batter."

Here is the batter.
It is in a bowl with a big spoon.

Harry is stirring the batter.
The spoon goes round
and round.
The batter goes round
and round.

Oops!
There is more
batter outside
the bowl than inside!

Harry's mother says, "I think that is enough stirring, Harry. I will finish making the cake now. Perhaps you can help Grandpa."

Harry likes to help Grandpa.
Harry goes downstairs
to the basement.

There is Grandpa.
He is making
a model ship.

"Hi, Grandpa,"
says Harry.
"Can I help you?"

"Sure, Harry, you can help me," says Grandpa.
"I need someone to help me glue these little pieces together.
Would you like to do that?"

"Oh, yes" says Harry.

First, Harry puts glue on one piece. Then he puts glue on another piece. Then he sticks the two pieces together.

What fun!

The glue tickles Harry's nose.
It itches and itches.
Harry feels as if he is going
to sneeze.

"No, Harry!
Don't sneeze!"
shouts Grandpa.

Too late. Harry sneezes so hard he blows
all the little pieces right off the table.

There are pieces on the wall. There are pieces on the floor. There are even little pieces stuck in Grandpa's beard.

"I'm sorry, Grandpa," says Harry.

"Oh, that's all right, Harry.
Everyone sneezes now
and then.

But I think I know how you can be
the most help of all.
Come upstairs
with me."

First, Grandpa goes in the kitchen
and whispers something to Harry's mother.
Harry's mother smiles.

Then Grandpa whispers
something to Harry's father.
Harry's father smiles.

Then Grandpa whispers
something to Harry.
Harry smiles.

Can you guess what
Harry's grandfather whispered?

He said:
"We are going fishing.
Harry is going to help
keep me company."

Now Harry is the best helper of all!